Pug vs. Pug

Ahoy, mateys!

Set sail for a brand-new
adventure with the

#1 *Stowaway!*
#2 *X Marks the Spot*
#3 *Catnapped!*
#4 *Sea Sick*
Super Special #1 *Ghost Ship*
#5 *Search for the Sea Monster*
Super Special #2 *Best in Class*
#6 *Pug vs. Pug*

Coming soon:
Super Special #3 *Race to the North Pole*

PUPPY PIRATES

Pug vs. Pug

by Erin Soderberg
illustrations by Russ Cox

A STEPPING STONE BOOK™
Random House 🏠 New York

For my camping crew (Greg, Henry, Ruby,
Milla, Sarah, Jason, Nico, Max, Theo,
Christy, Steve, Andrew, Matthew, Anna, Jen,
Dave, Lily, and Abby), who have been fun
teammates on lots of wilderness adventures
—E.S.

Text copyright © 2017 by Erin Soderberg Downing and Robin Wasserman
Cover art copyright © 2017 by Luz Tapia
Interior illustrations copyright © 2017 by Russ Cox

Visit us on the Web!
randomhousekids.com
SteppingStonesBooks.com

Educators and librarians, for a variety of teaching tools, visit us at
RHTeachersLibrarians.com

Library of Congress Cataloging-in-Publication Data
Name: Soderberg, Erin, author.
Title: Pug vs. pug / Erin Soderberg ; interior illustrations by Russ Cox.
Other title: Pug versus pug
Description: New York : Random House, [2017] | Series: Puppy pirates ; #6 | Summary: Wally, Henry, and the rest of the pirate puppies are back for more adventures, this time dealing with some disagreeing pugs and a stranded situation.
Identifiers: LCCN 2016043246 | ISBN 978-1-5247-1410-9 (trade) | ISBN 978-1-5247-1411-6 (lib. bdg.) | ISBN 978-1-5247-1412-3 (ebook)
Subjects: | CYAC: Dogs—Fiction. | Pug—Fiction. | Pirates—Fiction. | Adventure and adventurers—Fiction. |
Classification: LCC PZ7.S685257 Pu 2017 | DDC [Fic]—dc23

Printed in the United States of America

10 9 8 7 6 5 4 3 2 1

First Edition

This book has been officially leveled by using the F&P Text Level Gradient™ Leveling System.

 CONTENTS

The Last Dinghy

"Anchors aweigh!" barked Captain Red Beard. "Load our loot into dinghies. Shake the sand off your fur. It's time for me crew to set sail!"

Puppies of all shapes and sizes raced across a sandy beach. They shook their bodies, scratched their ears, and rinsed their paws in salty ocean water. "Scratch hard, pups! Leave all the bugs here on shore," Red Beard ordered. Then he chuckled and added, "All the *pugs*, too."

Captain Red Beard's puppy pirate crew had spent the morning searching for buried treasure on a small island in the middle of the sea. They dug up three gold chests filled with tasty bones. Then they celebrated with an afternoon of swimming, chasing, and running. But now it was time to get back to their ship.

"Quickly!" Red Beard barked as pups climbed into the small wooden boats that would return them to their home on the water. "We must get back to the *Salty Bone* at once. The sun is sinking into the sea. When the sun goes underwater, that means night is here."

Wally, a soft golden retriever puppy, cocked his head. "Does the sun *really* go underwater, sir?"

"Aye, aye, *arrrr-oooo!*" Red Beard barked. "I've been a sailor for many years, little Walty. Every night, without fail, the sun plops into the ocean. Then it pops back up on the other side of the world the next morning." The gruff terrier lowered his voice and said, "This here is a fact, pup: the sun hides underwater at night and lights up the deep sea world."

Wally wasn't sure this was true. Sometimes Captain Red Beard mixed up his words and facts. But Wally didn't like to argue with his captain. Wally didn't like to argue with anyone, because it was no fun when other pups were upset with him. He was happiest when everyone got along.

"It's high time we set off on our next adventure!" Captain Red Beard said. He jumped into a dinghy just as it set off toward the *Salty Bone*. "Row carefully through these waters," the captain warned his crew. "There are sharp rocks and coral reefs hidden just below the ocean's surface. Keep a close lookout!"

Wally jumped into the last dinghy. Old Salt, a wise peg-legged Bernese mountain dog, was curled up at the front of the little boat. Wally's best mate, a human boy named Henry, hopped in and grabbed the oars.

Henry pointed at the pink-and-gold-streaked sky. "In case you were wondering, mates, a pink sky at night is a sailor's delight. It means good weather is ahead."

"And I've heard a pink sky in the morning means that sailors should take warning," Wally said, "because storms are coming. Is that legend true, Old Salt?"

Old Salt glanced at the pink sky. Then he pointed his paw at a bank of storm clouds gathering on the horizon. "I guess we'll find out, won't we?"

Henry was about to dip the oars into the water and push away from land when Captain Red Beard barked, "Avast!"

Wally's ears pricked. He could hear a worried tone in his captain's voice.

"I forgot something," Red Beard called out. This wasn't a surprise. The captain forgot lots of things. "I sent Curly, Wayne, and the pugs into the woods to gather coconuts. Little Walty, go fetch the last of our crew and help them carry the treats." He nodded toward the trees.

"Aye, aye, Captain," Wally barked back. He jumped out of the dinghy and raced across the sand.

Henry chased after him, calling, "Wait up, mate. Wait for me!"

"Better hustle, little Walty!" the captain howled from way offshore. He squinted at the sun, which was sinking into the sea. "The sun is almost all wet, and the waters around this island are too rocky to row through after dark!"

Wally and Henry ran as fast as their legs could go. The jungle forest was bright and cheerful during the day. But now that it was getting dark, Wally noticed that the trees cast spooky shadows.

Not far off, Wally could hear the pug sisters yipping at each other. Wally zipped through the brush. He burst into a clearing. The grassy, open space was lined with beautiful palm trees that hung heavy with coconuts. Wally had tasted coconut a few times before. The meat was sweet and creamy, but the outside had funny little hairs that tickled his lips. Wally knew never to eat too much coconut, because that meant tummy trouble.

On one side of the clearing, Curly and Wayne were working together. Curly was the *Salty Bone*'s first mate. Wayne the Great Dane was the biggest pup on their crew. Curly and Wayne made a perfect coconut-picking team. When Curly stood on Wayne's back, she could reach the lowest coconuts on the trees. The pair had filled nearly four rolling crates to bring back to their ship.

Piggly and Puggly hadn't filled a single crate. Instead, the pugs had found a way to make mischief. "Wally!" Piggly yelped. "Want to try our coconut collector?"

"Look, they made a trampoline!" Henry exclaimed. Using ropes twisted around a cluster of springy branches, the two little pugs had created a bouncy platform. They were taking turns jumping high into the air.

"It's time to get back to the ship," Wally barked to his crewmates. "Captain says we have to hurry!" Curly and Wayne howled to show they had heard him. But the pugs were yapping too loudly to hear the orders.

Piggly soared into the air, snagged a coconut, and tossed it to the ground. Then Puggly took her turn. They jumped and tossed, over and over again. Coconuts rolled across the ground. Piggly announced that she could jump the highest. Puggly yipped that she could toss the farthest. Piggly said she was best at breaking the coconuts when she tossed them. Puggly claimed she was best at hitting a target.

"Hey, pugs!" Wally shouted. The trees' shadows were growing longer and darker by the minute. "We really need to go or we'll be stranded!"

"One last jump," Piggly snorted. She barked to her sister, "Me, then you."

At the same time, Puggly howled, "Me, then you!"

The two pugs jumped high into the air together. They crashed into each other. They thrashed. They snarled. And then they fell.

Down.

Down.

Down.

Ker-plop! The two chubby pugs tumbled into Curly and Wayne's crates, sending hundreds of furry fruits flying.

The Coconut War

"I said, *me*, then you!" Piggly snapped.

"And *I* said, me, then *you!*" Puggly growled back.

"I said it first," wailed Piggly.

"No, *I* said it first," snapped Puggly.

"Our coconuts!" moaned Wayne. The Great Dane hung his huge head sadly. Then he plunked his big behind down on the grass.

"This is all your fault, Puggly," Piggly snapped. "You *always* want to be first."

"*I* always want to be first? You budge in line for everything!" howled Puggly. Wally looked from pug to pug. Puggly was sort of right. Piggly was often first in line for all the fun stuff they did as a crew. But she hung back at the end of the line when it was time for work or chores. Puggly glared at her sister and said, "Special outings, meals, snack time—"

Piggly cut her sister off and snarled, "I eat before you because you're always late! You get too busy styling your fur and putting on your fancy outfits. It's your own fault you end up last in line."

Puggly snuffed angrily. Wally thought Piggly kind of had a point, too. Puggly loved fancy things, and some of her special outfits did take a very long time to put on. She was a slowpoke when there were mirrors and costumes to distract her.

"I'm sure I heard *Puggly* say she would jump first," Curly said. She stepped forward to try to settle the argument, like the top-notch first mate she was. "Piggly, you should apologize."

Wayne cocked his head. "I heard *Piggly* first, loud and clear. I think Puggly should say she's sorry."

Curly and Puggly growled at Piggly. "This is your fault," Puggly snapped. "Arrrr you going to clean up the mess you made, you scalawag?"

Wayne and Piggly glared back at Puggly. "You must be barking mad! It's *your* fault," Piggly said, her gold tooth glinting. She snarled, "Better get to work stacking these coconuts in the crates."

"It's your fault!"

"No, it's *your* fault!"

Wally's and Henry's heads whipped back and forth while the two pairs of dogs growled and yapped at each other. Then Wally put his head between his paws and covered his ears. He hated seeing his friends fight!

He also hated to think how angry Captain Red Beard would be if they returned to the ship with empty crates. These coconuts meant many weeks of special treats! But they were still scattered all over the ground.

Since his friends were busy fighting, Wally decided to pick up the coconuts himself. As his friends' barks rang out around him, Wally dropped furry fruits gently into the crates,

one by one. But even after Henry started to help, it was clear it would take a while to fill the four crates again.

Before long, Wally could hardly see the coconuts on the ground. The sky was much darker now, and the brown balls blended into the shadows. He glanced up. The moon was glowing overhead. The sun was no longer painting the sky pink—the dome above them was just a smooth, dark blue. What if they were already too late to load up the dinghy?

"Here you are!" boomed a loud voice from somewhere nearby. Wally snapped to attention. It was Old Salt. "Quit your fightin'," the old dog warned in his low, rumbling voice.

"Aye," Wally agreed. "We need to get back to the dinghy right away."

"What about our coconuts?" wailed Wayne.

"Ya have to leave 'em," Old Salt said, turning

toward the beach. "I came out here to tell you there's no time to waste."

With a huff, Piggly said to Wayne, "Will you tell Puggly I'm *not* sharing my coconut with her, even if she says she's sorry?" She snatched a coconut up in her mouth and glared at her sister.

Puggly held her tail high and turned her back to Piggly. She glanced at Curly and said, "And will *you* tell Piggly I'm not talking to her?"

Piggly grunted. Then she and Wayne trotted out of the clearing behind Old Salt, each with a coconut clutched tightly in their mouth. Puggly and Curly waited a moment, then followed at a distance. Wally and Henry took up the rear.

The group moved quickly. But by the time they reached the beach, the sun was already completely underwater. It was too dark to row through the rocky waters around the island. And it was too dark for anyone from the *Salty Bone* to come back and get them. The water was off-limits until morning.

"In case you were wondering, mates?" Henry said, gazing out at the dark sea. "We are stranded."

Survival 101

"There's no need to worry," Old Salt said in a soothing voice. "I've been a pirate all me life. I know just what we need to survive a night on land."

Wally whimpered. He had spent plenty of nights on dry land as a small pup. But he had gotten used to sleeping in his own bunk out at sea, surrounded by the rest of the crew. Every night, he fell asleep curled inside his blanket, with the creaking and gentle swaying of the ship lulling him into dreamland. How could he make it through the night without the sounds and smells of home?

"We'll make an adventure out of this!" Henry announced. "We can set up a shelter, build a fire, and tell each other stories!"

Wally tried to get excited. Henry was right: this could be a fun adventure. He and some of his best mates had a whole island to themselves! The only trouble was the coconut crew was still arguing. It didn't sound like they were in the mood for telling silly stories.

"I hope you're happy with yourself," Piggly snapped at Puggly. "All because of you, we're stuck on this island all night *without any dinner!*"

Puggly sat down with her back to her sister. She blinked at Curly and said, "Will you tell Piggly it's her *own* fault she's missing dinner?"

Curly passed along the message in a snippy voice.

Wayne stepped forward and grunted, "You really need to say you're sorry, Puggly."

Puggly poked her tongue out. "How about you mind your own business, ya scurvy dog?"

Old Salt stepped between the two groups of pups. "Shiver me timbers, I have never heard so much nonsense in me life! Does it really matter who is to blame?"

For a moment, silence settled over the group. Piggly looked at Puggly. Puggly looked at Piggly. Then, at the same time, both of them barked, "*Yes!*"

Old Salt shook his head. "Tonight, you're all going to be too busy for blame," he warned them. "There are some basic things we need to do to survive in the wild. First, we should build a shelter that will protect us from the wind and rain if a storm comes. We have to be sure it's far enough from the sea that the tide won't wash it away."

Piggly muttered something under her breath to Puggly. Puggly poked her sister with her tail.

"Aye, aye," Wally said loudly. He wanted Old Salt to know that *someone* was listening.

"And every pup needs plenty of freshwater," Old Salt went on. "Salt water isn't safe to drink—it just makes a pup thirstier. So we should search for a source of freshwater, or it will be a mighty long night."

Curly shook sand out of her fur . . . straight into Wayne's eyes. He growled at her.

"Aye, aye!" Wally repeated, even louder.

"Though we don't *need* food till tomorrow, a bite to eat might make everyone much happier," Old Salt added. "So finding food will be another task for our crew."

"What about coconuts?" Wally asked. "There are lots of coconuts!"

"There would have been, if Piggly hadn't ruined everything," Puggly said.

Piggly grunted. "You're the one who—"

"Too much coconut causes tummy trouble for pups," Old Salt reminded them. "We'll need more food than that."

"In case you were wondering," Henry said, "we will need to build a fire to keep warm. I'm great at starting fires. Wanna see?"

Old Salt barked his approval. So Henry worked on starting the fire. Meanwhile, Wally

and the other pups started building a shelter.
First, they gathered as many large sticks and
branches as they could find. Using a fallen tree
as their base, they created a little roof out of the
branches.

No one was talking, which wasn't very fun.
But at least no one was *fighting*. Wally was grate-
ful for that.

Then Wayne decided to test out their fort.
The huge pup was much too large for the shelter.
When Wayne squirmed under the branches,
the whole thing toppled over.

Curly snapped at Wayne, "Now who owes everyone an apology?"

Wayne drooped. "It's not my fault you're building a shelter that only fits little scrawny dogs."

Curly growled at Wayne. Though she was tiny, Curly was fierce. And she did *not* like others making fun of her size. "I order you to take that back, you big beast!"

"No," Wayne barked. "I won't."

"You will!" Curly yipped.

Piggly stood beside Wayne, while Puggly joined Curly. The pups faced off and started barking and howling at each other all over again.

Old Salt woofed for attention. Somewhere off in the distance, a rumble of thunder echoed. All the pups pricked their ears and settled down. "The key to survival is teamwork," Old Salt said sternly. "How can you call yourselves a crew if you can't figure out how to get along?"

Wally looked around nervously at his friends. He got along with all of them. Why couldn't they stop fighting?

Old Salt was a kind dog, but he could be stern when he wanted to. One by one, Piggly, Puggly, Wayne, and Curly turned away from the old pup. They fixed their eyes on the ground. Curly seemed embarrassed. Wayne was sad. Piggly and Puggly were probably hungry.

But Piggly and Puggly were *always* hungry.

Finally, Piggly barked, "Maybe Old Salt is right."

Wally breathed a sigh of relief. His friends were ready to call a truce!

"Aye, Old Salt *is* right," Puggly agreed. "We can't be a crew. Not anymore. For the rest of this night, we'll be *two* crews. Starting now."

Pug vs. Pug

"From now on, it's pug versus pug," Piggly said, growling.

Wayne stood behind her and announced, "I'm on Team Piggly."

Puggly snorted. "Good luck with that."

"Team Puggly, for the win!" barked Curly. She and Puggly stood shoulder to shoulder.

"What about you, Wally?" Piggly asked.

"Yeah, what about you?" Puggly barked.

Wally whimpered. He pawed at the ground. How was he supposed to choose between his friends?

The pups got tired of waiting for Wally to answer. They marched off in opposite directions. On one end of the beach, Piggly and Wayne started dragging sticks to make a shelter for their camp. Puggly and Curly huddled together at the other end of the beach, barking quietly as they hatched a plan.

Wally stood frozen between the two camps, wondering what to do. "How can I pick a side?" Wally asked Old Salt.

"You don't," said Old Salt. "I don't plan to."

"But what *can* I do?" Wally groaned. He swung his head back and forth, watching Team Piggly and Team Puggly work on their shelters. Thanks to Wayne, Team Piggly had size and strength—the enormous Great Dane was very big and super tough. He had already pulled dozens of huge sticks out of the woods. He and Piggly were building a tall wooden tent.

Though they weren't big, Team Puggly had plenty of smarts—Curly was very clever. In fact, she was one of the smartest pups on Captain Red Beard's crew. That's what made her a great first mate. Instead of using branches to build a shelter from scratch, Curly and Puggly found a rock pile at the back of the beach. Curly sniffed out a small, cavelike space between the rocks, big enough for the pups to burrow into.

"Come join us!" Curly called to Wally. "It's nice and warm in here."

"Want to test out our tepee, Wally?" Wayne asked, poking his head around a wall of branches.

Wally sat down on his haunches and refused to move. "I have good mates on both teams! Why can't they just work together?" he asked Old Salt.

The wise pirate shook his head. "You can't force everyone to get along, Wally. Sometimes pups just need a little time and space to figure out how much they need each other."

"What are we supposed to do until they figure that out?" Wally asked. Thunder boomed somewhere out at sea.

Henry was still trying to start a fire. The rumbling made him squint up at the sky. "In case you were wondering, I think that storm's getting closer," he said.

Wally's fur stood up on his shoulders, which meant the storm was nearby. He remembered the old sailing legend: *Pink sky at night is a sailor's delight. Pink sky in the morning, sailors take warning.* So much for that! It was quickly becoming clear that this night would *not* be much of a delight.

"Until they figure it out, we wait," said Old Salt, heaving himself to his feet. Then he hobbled across the beach, away from the shore.

"Where are you going?" Wally yelped.

"I'm going to take a walk in the jungle. I could use some peace and quiet after listening to these young pups sniping at each other all afternoon." Old Salt shuffled slowly to the edge of the trees. "I'm also going to look for some freshwater. No sense sitting around, waiting for those pups to remember they need it."

"Should I come with you?" Wally asked.

"You're the only one who listened to me about survival," Old Salt said. "I have a feeling your friends might need your help here on the beach."

Wally didn't want to be left alone with his fighting friends. But he knew Old Salt was right. He watched the old dog shuffle away down the beach. Soon Old Salt had melted into the forest shadows. Wally and Henry were on their own. In the middle of a pug war.

Survival of the Fluffiest

"Wally!" Piggly called. "We need your help!"

"Wally!" Puggly shouted. "Come lend us a paw!"

Wayne yelped, "Wally, how do you—?"

Curly woofed, "Wally, don't you think we should—?"

Wally raced back and forth between the two camps. He repeated everything he had learned from Old Salt. He wanted to be sure all his friends were aware of their basic needs for survival: water, food, fire, and shelter.

Nearly an hour after the sun had set, Henry finally managed to get a fire started. As soon as the embers erupted into flames, Piggly and Wayne called the fire for themselves. "Henry built the fire on our side of the beach, so that means it belongs to *our* team," Piggly said loudly.

Wally didn't think that was fair.

But he *did* think Team Piggly needed some source of heat. The shelter Wayne and Piggly had built was nothing more than a fragile lean-to made of sticks and bamboo. Pieces of the tent kept falling over or snapping in half. Whenever the wind whipped sand across the beach, the stick fort did nothing to protect the two pups.

With their short, wiry coats, both Wayne and Piggly got cold much more quickly than either Wally or Curly did in chilly weather. Having poodle or retriever fur was like wearing a blanket at all times —Wally's fluffy coat kept him warm, even when he was soaking wet. Team

Puggly would be warm and dry in the little cave they made for themselves. But if it rained, Team Piggly would be very cold indeed.

"In case you were wondering," Henry said, after inspecting Piggly and Wayne's stick fort, "the other two pups made their shelter out of—"

"Avast!" Piggly barked to cut him off. "We don't want to know what those scurvy dogs are doin'."

"Aren't you cold?" Wally asked. He wanted to tell Team Piggly how the other two pups had dug holes in the sand and piled up leaves to create warm beds inside their cave. He wouldn't mention the fact that Puggly had even decorated the cave with some of the ribbons from her fur.

Wayne howled, refusing to listen. "The cold doesn't bother us. We're tough, unlike those wimpy kittens."

"And you can tell them that *we* have full bellies," Piggly bragged. "Wayne waded into the ocean and caught us plenty of fish for dinner. A tummy full of fish is all I need."

"You can have as much of our fish as you want," Wayne offered. "Just join Team Piggly!"

Wally looked out at the dark sea. The waves crashed loudly on the beach. Only a big dog like Wayne could brave that water. Curly and Puggly were both too small to risk it. Where would they get food for their dinner?

He trotted across the beach to check on his other friends. Curly and Puggly were very hungry . . . but they were also very warm. Their shelter was well protected from the wind and any rain that might come.

"Look what we found!" Curly bragged. She showed Wally a small freshwater stream trickling behind their cave. "Now we have water to drink *and* a dry place to sleep. Not like those

foolish pups on Team Piggly. We have everything we need."

Then Puggly's stomach growled loudly.

"Well, almost everything," Curly added.

"We could share a coconut," Puggly suggested.
"If we followed our tracks from earlier today
into the woods, I'm sure we could find the crates
of coconuts."

"Eating coconut on an empty belly is a bad idea for pups," Curly reminded her partner. "Coconut is a great treat *with* something else, but it's not a meal."

Puggly groaned. "I'm starvin', Curly."

"Drink up," Curly told her. "If you have enough water, your tummy will be fooled into thinking it's full."

"My tummy might be fooled, but my brain won't!" Puggly moaned. The smell of delicious roasted fish was wafting across the beach from the fire. "If I don't get something to eat soon, I'm gonna die."

Curly cocked her head. "You won't *die*. You might not have much energy, but you'll make it through the night."

"I'm not so sure about that," Puggly whimpered.

Wally hated to see his friend so sad . . .

even if it was her own fault. It didn't make any sense for Puggly and Curly to go hungry, when the other half of their crew had so much to eat.

"I can ask Piggly and Wayne to share some of the fish they caught," Wally said. "There's more than enough for everyone."

"We don't want *anything* from those scalawags!" Puggly grunted.

"Aye!" Curly snapped. "We are much better off on our own. Have you *seen* their shelter? It's a joke!"

Wally sighed. It was hard being stuck in the middle. He wished all his friends could get along.

"In case you were wondering?" Henry said quietly to Wally. He pointed toward Wayne and Piggly. "I just realized *that* camp has food and fire, but no water or true shelter." Then he nodded in the direction of Puggly and Curly.

"And *that* camp has freshwater and shelter, but no food or fire."

"Aye," Wally said as thunder rumbled overhead. He realized something else, too. He and Henry had no food, no water, *and* no shelter. If they didn't pick a side soon, they were in for a cold, wet night.

Fish or Water

"*Yum yum yum yum yum!*" Piggly taunted from her place near the fire. "This fish is delish."

Puggly groaned. Then she said to Curly, "Will you tell Piggly that I can't hear her?"

"If I tell her that," Curly pointed out, "she'll know you *can* hear her."

Near the fire, Wayne licked fish off his paws and stretched his back. Glancing over at Team Puggly, he barked, "Ah, that was a feast. I haven't eaten such a tasty meal in weeks."

Piggly giggled. "Aye, Steak-Eye's stew is nothing compared to freshly caught fish." She leaned toward Wayne and said quietly, "But I sure am thirsty after that big meal!"

Over on the other side of the beach, Wally heard Curly say to Puggly, "Even Steak-Eye's stew sounds delicious right about now. My belly is mighty empty."

Puggly groaned in agreement. Then she raised her voice and barked, "Hey, Curly! Should we go drink up more of that cold, clear water? It tastes like gold compared to the old, stale water on board the *Salty Bone*."

"Aye, Puggly," agreed Curly. Her voice was just loud enough that Team Piggly could hear her perfectly.

Wally felt bad for his hungry and thirsty friends. Piggly had given him a taste of the delicious fish. And Puggly had let him lap up some sips of the freshwater. Now if only he could get the two teams to share with *each other*!

"We should probably settle into our snuggly shelter," Curly told Puggly, loudly enough so everyone could hear. "Looks like a storm's coming!"

Piggly wriggled her body by the fire and called out, "Our fire sure is warm and cozy, Wayne. Much better than a smelly shelter, don't you think?"

Wally tucked his head between his paws and whined. He didn't like the way his friends were acting. Now they were being mean to each other! This fight had gone on long enough. Just as Wally was about to say something, the sky opened and huge drops of rain poured down. Curly and Puggly ducked into their shelter. They peeked out the mouth of the cave, looking to see what the others would do in the storm.

Piggly and Wayne were quickly soaked. Wind whipped at their shelter and sent bamboo rods flying.

"In case you were wondering," Henry yelled, "that whole thing is about to go over!" Everyone watched as the raging wind blew Team Piggly's shelter down.

"Who needs a shelter when you have a nice, toasty fire to stay warm?" Wayne said loudly as he and Piggly shivered beside the fire.

"Hey, mates, check this out!" Henry hollered. He dragged the small wooden dinghy toward the fire. "Look! Rain is collecting in the bottom of the dinghy. Is anyone thirsty for some freshwater?"

Wayne and Piggly raced toward the boat. They climbed inside and lapped up the water on the bottom. Piggly glared at her sister and said, "Ha! Now *both* camps have water. Score one for Team Piggly!"

"And we have fire!" bragged Wayne. "And food. So it looks like the winner of *this* survival game is Team Piggly! Fire, food, and water."

"You don't have shelter," snapped Puggly. Then she quickly turned her back to him and yapped, "What I meant to say is: Curly, will you remind those two scurvy dogs that they don't have shelter?"

At that moment, Curly let out three short warning barks. Puggly spun around in time to see the fire fizzle out. The rain had soaked it completely.

"At least we still have full bellies," grunted Piggly. "Plus, we all have water. You wimpy fluffballs can curl up in your cat's nest and hack up a hair ball for dinner. We'll keep eatin' our fishy feast over here."

Puggly groaned quietly. "Aw, Curly. Even a hair ball sounds tasty right about now."

"Well, we don't have a hair ball," Curly reminded her. "We have water and a beautiful shelter. That's got to be enough."

Wayne moaned. "We've got water and food. But I'd give anything for a dry bed, Piggly. It will be a mighty long night out here in the rain."

"Too bad," Piggly sighed. She glanced over at the remains of their lean-to. Her small ears were pressed flat against her head, weighed down by all the rain. "Mate, the only place we have to sleep tonight is a puddle of mud."

"This is a disaster," Wally moaned to Henry. *If only Captain Red Beard were here,* Wally thought. *Then he could* order *the crew to get along.* Wally couldn't order anyone to do anything. He would have to convince his friends they *wanted* to stop fighting.

But how?

Two Plus Two Equals More

"Enough is enough," Wally barked. It was time to fix this.

"In case you were wondering, mate?" Henry said, giggling. He brushed his hand across his face to wipe away the rainwater. "You are very skinny when you're all wet."

Wally couldn't help but smile. Life was always more fun if he could find something to laugh about ... especially if he wasn't having the best time. Wally's soft, downy, golden fur was usually fluffy. But now his hair was soaked through. It would take hours to dry. Most of the time, Wally had sunshine or a cozy blanket to help him dry off after taking a swim or getting caught in the rain. Tonight, he had neither. He hung his head and sighed. "Everyone is either wet or hungry. This campout isn't fun at all."

He wanted to crawl into the cave with Puggly and Curly, but that would upset Piggly and Wayne. And he wanted more fish to help him keep his mind off the cold, but that would upset Puggly and Curly. Wally couldn't stand to make anyone unhappy. Especially when they were already so unhappy.

He could hear Wayne's soft whines coming from near the soaked fire. On the other side of the beach, Puggly was quietly groaning.

That's it! Wally thought. He suddenly knew how to make the pups *want* to get along.

Using his biggest voice, Wally barked out, "Listen up, mates! If we combine your two camps, then we can all have food *and* shelter. Team Piggly, you have more than enough food to share. Team Puggly, your cave would be even more snuggly with a bigger pile of pups."

"I don't want my pretty shelter to stink like wet dog," Puggly grumbled.

Wally ignored her. He knew that wasn't true. Though she loved pretty things, Puggly was rough-and-tumble and didn't let a little dirt or stink stand in her way—just like most of the pirates on their crew. These pups needed to remember that even without a ship, they were still pirates. They were still a *crew*.

"A good pirate knows when it's time to call a temporary truce," Wally barked at his friends.

"Hmm . . . there was that time Captain Red Beard called a truce with the kitten ship," Curly reminded Puggly.

"It was the only way to defeat the great Sea Slug," Wayne told Piggly.

"If puppies and kittens can get along for one day, then surely you can get along for one *night*," Wally added.

There was a long silence. Wally crossed his paws for luck. This had to work.

Finally, Piggly barked, "Aye. We'll share our fish—but only because we don't want it to rot before we have time to eat it all."

"And we'll share our shelter," Puggly snapped. "But only if you tell Piggly she has to say sorry."

"I won't say sorry!" Piggly said. "Unless you say: Please, Piggly, can I have some of your fish . . . you strong, clever, best-pirate-in-all-the-seven-seas sister of mine?"

Puggly huffed. "I'll say no such thing."

"Silence!" Wally barked. He was afraid this truce would be over before it began. "No one is allowed to talk. We'll eat, we'll sleep, and then it will be morning and we can all go home to the *Salty Bone*."

Wally couldn't believe it, but the crew did exactly what they were told! All the pups huddled together inside Team Puggly's shelter. They were very squished. But the rocky space

was mostly protected from the rain. And all those bodies jammed together quickly helped everyone stop shivering. So did filling their bellies with delicious fish.

No one said a word. Wally was surrounded by his friends—but this was the loneliest meal he'd ever had. He wished there was some way to turn the night into a fun campout on the beach, with stories and songs and silly games. But with so much fighting, they would be lucky to survive the night.

"I've got an idea," Henry said, after too many long minutes of silence. He scrambled out of the shelter. The five pups watched as the boy pulled the little dinghy toward the cave. He flipped the small wooden boat and balanced it over the opening of the cave. Now Henry could stretch his legs out and still be protected from the rain. "I just turned this cave into the best shelter ever!"

"Aye," Wally agreed. "We could fit half our crew in here if we needed to."

Suddenly, Curly poked her nose into the air. "Something's not right," she said, alert.

Wayne lifted his heavy head off his paws, looked around, and blinked. "You're right," he said. "Someone's missing."

"Piggly?" Puggly barked, making sure her sister was still in the cave.

"Puggly?" Piggly barked at the same time.

Both pugs wagged their tails in relief. Even though they were fighting, it was obvious they were still looking out for each other—at least a little bit.

Wally yelped. "Old Salt!"

"Where is he?" Piggly asked. "I thought he was in the cave with Puggly."

"Will you tell Piggly that I thought Old Salt was with her?" Puggly snorted. "I figured she and Wayne needed the old dog's help if they were going to have any hope of survivin' the night."

"If he's not with us," Curly barked, "and he's not with you . . . then where is he?"

Wally jumped up. "He went for a walk in the woods!" The pug war had kept Wally so busy that he had forgotten about him. The old dog was so smart that no one ever really worried about him. But he had been gone for hours. "What if—" Wally gulped. "What if something happened to him?"

Monkey Business

The group spilled out of the shelter and raced
across the beach. With their bellies full, they had
much more energy. They were also happy to find
that the rain had slowed. Now there was just a
light mist—small drops of water glittering in the
moonlight. The air was cool, causing steam to
rise off the calm, dark surface of the sea.

Together, the five pups and Henry made their
way to the edge of the beach and trudged into the
jungle. The pups put their noses to the ground

and sniffed to search for the old dog's trail. But the rain had washed away nearly every smell.

"Old Salt!" Wally called.

"*Arrrr-oooo!*" Curly howled. "Old Salt!"

"Old Salt, ol' pal!" barked Wayne.

"Old Salt!" Piggly and Puggly yipped at exactly the same time. Then, together again, they said, "Jinx!" For a moment, the twin sisters grinned at each other. But as soon as they remembered they were still fighting, both pugs snarled and turned in opposite directions.

For a long while, the group of six walked between dense trees and through long grass. They hopped over fallen logs, scratched their backs on the trunks of palm trees, and stopped to lap up water at a narrow freshwater stream they crossed.

Along the way, all five puppies howled and barked, crying out for their missing crewmate. Sticks cracked under their paws. Small animals scattered. Bugs nipped at their bodies. Birds called *ka-chee ka-chee ka-chee!* There was no sign of Old Salt anywhere.

When the group stopped for a short rest in a clearing, Wally looked up and spotted a colorful toucan gazing down at them from atop a

feathery-looking tree. It screamed *rrrrk rrrrk rrrrk!* The noise was so funny that the others craned their necks to see the colorful bird that was making such silly sounds.

Piggly kept trying to copy the toucan's call, but it sounded more like she was choking on a hair ball. Then Puggly took her turn, but she ended up sneezing with laughter. The toucan stared back at both of the pugs. Then she called *rrrk rrrk* again before flying away over the canopy of trees.

When they set off, Henry picked up a walking stick to help clear a path through the large, heavy leaves. He laughed as drops of rainwater rolled off the leaves and spilled down onto the group. It turned into a sort of game, with the puppies bounding playfully out of the way to avoid the spray.

Before long, Henry's swinging stick woke a family of beasts tucked into the highest branches of a huge tree. Dozens of furry, long-legged creatures leaped out of the treetops and howled at the group. There were at least twenty of them, all wailing and making terrible sounds.

Wally jumped behind Henry to hide. But the creatures had them surrounded.

"Monkeys!" yelped Wayne, screeching to a stop. "Maybe the monkeys on this island took Old Salt and are keeping him as their prisoner?"

"I don't think that's what happened," Wally said, noticing that the monkeys seemed to be keeping their distance.

Curly agreed. "Old Salt could probably talk his way out of a trap like that. He's been around a long time, and he's never been anyone's prisoner. He's very sly."

"In case you were wondering," Henry said wisely, "howler monkeys are no threat. They eat leaves, fruit, nuts, and flowers."

"They're not gonna eat us, but they sure are noisy. This crew is makin' enough noise to wake the whole jungle!" Curly said.

"*Ah-woo!*" Piggly said, copying the monkeys. She wiggled her short legs like the monkeys were doing. Seeing her sister act like a howler monkey made Puggly fall over in a fit of giggles.

Puggly sang out, "*Arrrr-oooo!*" Then she swished her short, curly tail back and forth. Soon all the monkeys were dancing and jumping around with the pups. The forest echoed with howls and wails.

Wayne joined in, crooning, "*Ooooooold Salllllt!*"

Curly barked. "We're supposed to be looking for Old Salt," she scolded. "Not singing like monkeys."

Everyone quieted down. Once again, the pugs remembered that they were supposed to be fighting—not goofing off. Piggly growled and pointed her paw to the east. "Let's go this way."

But Puggly planted her feet in the ground and looked west. "No, let's go *this* way."

Everyone started fighting again. They were all barking and growling in their loudest voices. The monkeys were still howling. And that's when Wally realized something. "Avast!" he barked. "We have been making so much noise that if Old Salt were calling back to us, we couldn't hear him."

The pugs glanced at each other. After a moment's consideration, they both nodded. "Wally's got a point," Piggly said.

"Aye," agreed Puggly.

"Let's try again," Wally said, once the monkeys had quieted down. "But this time, we'll work together. Call, then wait."

Following Wally's orders, they called Old Salt's name again. Wally went first, and then the whole group listened to see if they could hear an answer. They walked a bit farther before Curly tried. Then Wayne took his turn. After walking a little more, Puggly howled, "Old Salt!"

Finally, after another twenty paces of silence, Piggly yelled, "Old Salt!"

They listened once more. And that's when they heard him shouting. The group charged through the woods toward the sound of their mate's voice. At first, it was faint—but soon they could hear him more clearly. "Up here!" the old dog barked.

The group skidded to a stop and looked up . . . to find Old Salt, stuck in a tree.

Setting Things Right

"What in the name of Growlin' Grace are you doing in a *tree*?" Curly barked.

"In case you were wondering," Henry said loudly, "dogs don't climb trees. That's more of a cat thing."

"Are you callin' Old Salt a *kitten*?" Puggly growled.

"Take it back!" Piggly snapped.

Though Wally didn't like to see anyone upset with his best mate, he was happy to see the

two pugs agree about something again. "You know that's not what Henry meant," Wally said. He stepped forward to defend his human. "I think he was just wondering the same thing as Curly. What *are* you doing up in that tree, Old Salt?"

Old Salt coughed. "It doesn't matter how I ended up here," he said. Then, in a weary voice, he added, "You pups shouldn't be asking how things went wrong . . . but rather, how to set them right."

"Huh?" Wayne asked, cocking his head.

"How to set things right?" Wally repeated. He was confused, too.

"Many things have gone wrong tonight," Old Salt said. He shifted his gaze from Piggly and Wayne to Puggly and Curly. It was clear to everyone that he was talking about much more than being stuck in a tree. "We don't need to focus too hard on how any of this happened. The most important thing is to figure out how to make it right again . . . and how we move on from here."

"Aye," Piggly and Puggly said at the same time. With a giggle, both pugs added, "Jinx!"

"I said it first!" Piggly sneezed.

"No, *I* said it first," Puggly grunted.

After staring each other down, Piggly suggested, "Maybe we could just call it a tie?"

"Aye," Puggly said happily. "A tie."

Curly and Wayne both barked, "Aye, a tie!" Everyone laughed.

Everyone except Old Salt. He cleared his throat loudly. "Maybe it's time we *all* move on from here."

At the sound of Old Salt's voice, the pups looked up. The ancient Bernese mountain dog was still clinging to his branch. He looked pretty funny up there. But he definitely was not laughing.

"So," Wally said, "does anyone have an idea for how we get our mate out of the tree?"

"Maybe he could just jump down?" suggested Puggly.

"He can't jump and risk a broken leg," Wayne pointed out. "He's already got one peg leg—he doesn't need three more."

"In case you were wondering? We could use my rope and some sticks to build a ladder the old dog could climb down," Henry announced.

He pulled a length of thin, strong rope out of his back pocket. "A good pirate always has the right supplies on hand."

While Henry got to work building a ladder, the rest of the crew stared at the tree. "How are we going to get the ladder to him?" Piggly asked. "He's a long way up there."

The tree's large trunk was smooth and clear of branches. Old Salt was more than ten feet up, much higher than Henry's arms could reach to secure the ladder. As soon as the simple ladder was ready, the boy tried shinnying up the tree to attach it. But without anything to hold on to, Henry kept sliding back down to the ground.

Next, Wayne held one end of the ladder in his mouth and stood on his hind legs. But even when he stretched as tall as he was able, he couldn't pass the ladder to their friend.

Piggly and Puggly slipped away from the group. They were whispering to each other.

Then Wally saw the two naughty pugs exchange silly grins. He had seen that look before. They were hatching some sort of plan!

Working quietly, the two little wrinkled pups gathered flexible stalks of bamboo and fallen tree branches. Then they tugged their collection to the base of Old Salt's tree.

"We have an idea!" Puggly announced.

"Anyone want to help?" Piggly asked.

The rest of the group followed the pugs' orders, gathering branches into a pile. Near the bottom of the tree, the two pugs used their snouts to push the thin branches into a long line.

"You're building another trampoline!" Henry exclaimed, as soon as it became clear what the pugs had planned. "So we can jump up to help him down?"

"Aye, aye, matey," Puggly said, winking. "Our coconut collector is good for collecting more than just coconuts! Tonight, we can use it to collect our pal!"

Henry helped the pugs tie and twist and weave stalks of bamboo between the branches. The task wasn't quick or easy, but pirates love a challenge. After a lot of hard work, the springy platform was ready.

Puggly bounced on the trampoline first to test it out. But it was soon clear she couldn't get enough height to reach the branch Old Salt was sitting on. "Piggly, you're the best jumper," she said. "You should try."

So Piggly climbed onto the platform and leaped as high as she could—which wasn't very high at all.

"What if you work together?" Wally suggested. "If you jump on opposite sides, you might both get higher." When the pugs tried this, they each bounced much better than they had alone. But they still couldn't reach Old Salt.

"Can I give it a go?" Henry asked, stepping forward. He tucked the homemade ladder under one arm and hopped up onto the trampoline. After only a few tries, Henry bounced high enough that he could touch Old Salt's belly.

"Grab on to the branch!" Wayne howled. "Jump!"

"You're almost there!" Curly barked.

"*Arrrr-oooo!*" Wally cheered.

"Go, Henry!" Piggly and Puggly yelped together.

Henry's next jump was just enough that the boy was able to wrap his arm around the branch and swing up into the tree. "*Oof!*" Henry grunted. He hung the ladder on the branch and let the other end dangle toward the ground. Old Salt placed a huge front paw on the twisted mess of rope and branches, holding his peg leg off to one side. Then, stepping carefully so as not to lose his balance, Old Salt climbed down.

As soon as he saw that his mate was on solid ground, Henry dropped the ladder and slid off the branch onto the trampoline. *Bounce!*

The puppies cheered. Finally, their whole little crew was safe and sound—and together again.

Survival Stories

The jungle was no place to spend the night. So the crew scampered toward the beach. Finding their way back to camp was easy. This time, they could follow the trail of their own scents.

Now that the fight was over, there was no need for two camps. So the pups decided to make one giant super camp. Wayne fished for more food, while Puggly and Curly made Old Salt comfortable in the warmest part of the cave. Everyone would soon have food to eat, and there was plenty of freshwater to drink. If it rained again, they would be warm and dry.

Henry set to work starting another fire. Since all the wood on the beach was wet, it wasn't easy. Wally found some dry sticks inside the cave and dragged them out for his mate to use. Within minutes, Henry had a good fire crackling and roaring. It heated them up in no time.

Wayne trotted over to the fire and dropped a mouthful of freshly caught fish. Henry roasted them, and the smell was so tempting that Wally could hardly stand to wait for their snack. He was warm and cozy, his friends were safe and happy, and soon they would all have full bellies. Finally, they could truly enjoy a fun island sleepover.

The puppies sat in a circle around the fire. "Anyone want to hear a story while we wait for our dinner?" Henry asked, poking the roasting fish with a stick. There was a chorus of *ayes*.

Henry leaned forward, his eyes shining in the firelight. He told a silly tale about a group of friends, lost in the woods, who escaped from an angry tribe of howler monkeys. Wally giggled when he told them the star of the story was a pup named Henry.

By the time Henry reached the end, the fish was cooked perfectly. Piggly passed the first piece to Old Salt, then dropped the next piece at her sister's feet. "You, then me," she said.

Puggly nosed it back to her. "No, first *you,* then me."

Wayne stretched forward and snatched the fish off the ground. He flipped it into his mouth and said, "If you're gonna start that ol' argument again, *I'll* take the next piece. Thanks." The whole crew laughed.

"Aren't campouts supposed to have *scary* stories?" Piggly asked, licking the last morsels of fish off her paws.

"Aye!" barked Puggly. "And we've got a good one, don't we, Piggly?"

Piggly winked at her sister. "That we do," she said. Then, in a quiet, spooky voice, she began, "It was a dark and stormy night. The sea was angry."

"But the two brave pups weren't angry," Puggly added quickly. "They just wanted to make it
through the night together."

"Yeah," Piggly said, and gave her sister a
gentle shoulder bump. "They did everything together."

"Even fight ghosts!" Puggly barked. "And these were *biiiig* ghosts."

She and Piggly told a long story about a haunted island and the ghosts who lived there. Wally shivered. It sounded a lot like *this* island! He hid his face under Henry's leg and noticed that Wayne was leaning closer to Curly. It was nice to have friends to lean on when the world felt a little bit scary.

"There's one more story I want to hear," Piggly said as the first rays of morning sun stretched across the beach. "I think it's high time Old Salt told us how he got stuck up in that tree."

Old Salt laid his head on his paws and said nothing. He twitched his nose, and Wally thought he saw a little smile on his pal's face.

"Was it the monkey tribe?" Wayne suggested. "Did they pull you up with their tails?"

"Were you running from a toucan?" Puggly asked. "*Rrrrk rrrrk rrrrk!*"

"Or chasin' a critter?" Piggly suggested.

With a sly grin, Old Salt said, "That's quite a story"—he paused as a chorus of barks echoed from across the beach—"for another time."

Wally and his friends spilled out of the shelter, Old Salt's story forgotten. A fleet of dinghies had landed on the beach.

It was Captain Red Beard and some of the crew. They had come back for the stranded pups!

"Rise and shine, me barkies," Red Beard howled.

"We're saved!" Curly cheered. She raced across the beach to greet the puppy pirates who were leaping and bounding across the sand. Wayne, Henry, and the pugs all chased after her, eager to tell everyone stories about their night.

Wally hung back with Old Salt, hoping to hear his story. "Come on," Wally urged, walking slowly alongside his pal. "You can tell me. What really happened to you out there?"

"I'll share my tale in good time," Old Salt promised. "But for now, pup, let's get back to our ship. It's high time we collected more adventures that you can turn into stories of your own."

Wally howled, *"Arrrr-oooo!"* He definitely liked the sound of that!

All paws on deck!

Another Super Special Puppy Pirates
is on the horizon.
Here's a sneak peek at

Race to the North Pole

"Welcome to the North Pole!" Captain Red Beard barked to his crew. "As you all know, we have sailed through icy waters to run in the Great Ice Race. Teams of pups have come from all over the world to compete. Because the winner of the Great Ice Race wins the *greatest treasure of all!*"

"Treasure! Treasure! Treasure!" chanted the puppy pirates.

Curly, the first mate, barked for order. The

poufy mini poodle called out, "But there is a catch: the rules say we can only enter one team of six pups in the race."

"What is this hoodly-toodly nonsense? Only *six* pups?" howled the captain. He began to count his crew. "But we have one, two, three, forty-six, nineteen, eleven . . . fifty-two on our crew! Fifty-two is more than six. That is a problem."

"Every problem has a solution. Right, Captain?" Curly said, nodding. "And *you*, Captain, have come up with the perfect solution. A plan."

"Yes, of course!" Captain Red Beard said uncertainly. "I have a great plan. Remind me, what is my plan again?"

Curly faced the crew and said, "We have decided to hold a pre-race to find out who the fastest runners on our crew are. The five fastest pups will get to race with Captain Red Beard in the Great Ice Race."

"A pre-race!" Captain Red Beard said. "Yes, that is exactly what I was thinking. The first five pups to reach the finish line will be on my team. The rest of you will cheer us on."

Wally *loved* to run. He was very fast. He glanced around at his crewmates. There were many speedy and strong pups. Could Wally finish in the top five and earn the chance to race with his captain in the Great Ice Race?